A FESTIVE BLEND

Poetry Prose Pictures Puzzles

The Red Teapot Company

Compiled by Sue Shattock
Cover photographs: Marcia White
Editor: Nadya Henwood

Printed and bound in the UK.

ColourCafe Publishing
ISBN: 9781739995225

ABOUT

The Red Teapot Company was a concept formed in 2022 by Nadya Henwood and Sue Shattock and is an umbrella for all things creative.

After attending a play writing group at Chichester Festival Theatre, a small group of us started to meet regularly at the CFT cafe for a creative catch-up and to share our current and ongoing work. Many cups of tea and coffee later we still look forward to our monthly meetings and find inspiration, creative support and friendship in a convivial environment.

The Red Teapot Company now has three more members Marcia White, Avril J Evitts and Ken Hawkins (Biographies of all contributors are at back of the book). A Festive Blend is a collaborative collection of poetry, short stories and quizzes. It's an opportunity to share our work - this time it's on a Christmas theme.

So relax, pour yourself a cup of your preferred beverage and have a flick through. There is no specific order so you can dip in and out whenever you have time.

We all hope you have a wonderful Christmas and a very happy and healthy New Year.

Acknowledgements and Thanks

Many thanks to Jade Henwood for designing our lovely Red Teapot Logo.

A big thank you to Fortnum and Mason, 181 Piccadilly, St. James's, London W1A 1ER for their wonderfully imaginative Christmas Window Displays.

Thanks to Chichester Festival Theatre for their training programs, cafes, and creative environment.

CONTENTS - Photographs

CONTENTS - Poems, Prose and Puzzles

Getting ready for Christmas – Marcia
White

FESTIVAL OF LIGHT

Sue Shattock

I couldn't sleep, was wide awake,
Within the dead deep eve of night,
Thoughts raced around inside my head
And I longed for morning's light.

But then...

A moonbeam chinked through my curtain,
And slither-streamed across the floor.
Then, arrested in its bevelled glass reflection,
Threw joyful rainbows upon the bedroom door.

And glimmer-glinted the silver door handle,
Transforming all thoughts of gloom and doom,
As it illumined a cream sequinned jumper –
And spilled unexpected sparkles all around in my
room.

I think of it, as my midnight moonlit glitter ball,
A magical marvel of pure unexpected delight.
For just a moment, deep in the darkness,
I had my own brief/bright Festival of Light.

It was a Christmas gift I'll remember forever,
That single moonbeam that crept 'cross my floor;
Lighting up all the inky black darkness,
And all the rainbows that danced on the door.

This Way! – Marcia White

FLYING TO CHRISTMAS

Ken Hawkins

Normally, flying the regular route between Venus and Mars was a non-event, but not today. I was doing a loop around the moon when I started to pick up a strange sound, which I later came to know as earth music. I had no idea what this music meant but it went something like this 'Jingle bells, Jingle bells!'.

Earth people are interesting but slightly bizarre, so I thought I would take a closer look. I did another loop of the moon, got the trajectory right as I went into a lower orbit, when suddenly my scanner detected another craft on a collision course. I assumed it would take avoiding action but no, we bounced off one another. I ejected and landed in a pile of Christmas packages.

I was astonished when I saw the pilot was a large human with a white beard, dressed in a non-pressurised red suit. What was even more fascinating was his propulsion system. It was extraordinary, consisting of six large creatures with antennas protruding from their heads. These creatures were totally new to me.

Strange, but it was Christmas on earth!

Oh Christmas Tree – Marcia White

THE TREE DRESSING

Avril J Evitts

Julia called out to the children. Leo, Londo and Helena thundered down the stairs and gambolled into the living room, elbowing each other as they careered towards the tree.

Julia put on the old CD, 100 Best Ever Christmas Songs. Adjusting the volume, she tried to remember the ten best ever Christmas songs, let alone one hundred. To the strains of 'I Wish It Could Be Christmas Every Day', the children dived into boxes of lights, tinsel, beads and decorations.

Londo threw a garland of silver tinsel around Helena's head. He caught her arm,

'Leo, grab her, let's put her on the tree'.

Shrieks of delight mingled with pleas for help as Julia's dreams of an afternoon of reverie spent carefully choosing the right place for each ornament dissolved into the usual happy organised chaos of the annual tree dressing.

Helena struggled free and crawled under the dining table as the boys found their new favourite decorations. Londo dangled a mini-Darth Vader in Julia's face, 'This one first, pleeese'.

'No, no. Obi-Wan' demanded Leo. The two boys began to play fight and, complete with accompanying sound effects, they slashed and swished imaginary lightsabers at each other.

'The lights go first' came Helena's small but determined voice from the safety of her hideout.

'And the fairy last' said Julia as she carefully unwrapped the faded paper and delicately lifted the fairy, cradling it like a bird fallen from a nest.

Julia drifted into the memories of Christmases past. She could not remember a Christmas without the 1950s fairy, with her yellowing layers of gauze for a dress, mop of tangled blonde nylon hair and cardboard silver wings. When Julia and Peter moved in together Julia's mother had ceremoniously presented them with a tatty shoe box. 'Freya Fairy', as she had affectionately become known, lay with her sleeping eyes closed in a bed of ageing tissue paper. Julia was delighted, accepting the importance of this rite of passage. Peter less so, as he looked at the sorry state of this ancient relic.

Freya Fairy had lost her wand long ago. Julia had fashioned a new one out of a matchstick, foil and a silver bead. Julia had also woven a halo from red and gold thread to tame Freya Fairy's wild hair. Somehow, through the years, the wand

and halo had remained intact. Helena came and stood closely beside her mother.

'I think Helena should put Freya on the tree this year,' said Julia, 'We've had Freya...'

'Since forever' interrupted Londo, anxious to get to the fun part of switching on the lights. Leo already sat with a mass of tangled wires in his lap. There was always the exciting prospect of a fizz followed by a pop if a bulb blew, even better, a flash and bang as the main fuse plunged the house into darkness.

Londo picked up Obi-Wan and taunted Leo, 'Obi-Wan's going to die'. Leo dumped the lights and charged after Londo as he ran upstairs. Seconds later there were thumps, crashes, and cries from the boys' bedroom. Helena looked at Julia and there passed between them signs of both resignation and dismay. 'Here, hold Freya Fairy, I'll go and sort them out'.

Helena stood gazing at the fragile fairy, so much bigger in her small hands. She wished her mother would hurry up with the boys and come and take this precious cargo from her. Helena gently tilted the doll and Freya Fairy's eyes opened.

'Hello, hello' shouted Freya excitedly 'Oh my, how you have grown'. But no matter how loud Freya shouted, no one heard her tiny tinkling voice above the music. Freya carried on regardless, 'Where are the boys? Who is putting me on top of the tree this year, the tree, the tree, it is real isn't it?'

She had a thousand and one questions that could all be answered now, if only someone could hear her. From 60 years' experience she knew that over the next couple of days the answers would become apparent as she sat in her vantage point, silently observing from the top of the tree. Reluctantly, she allowed her eyes to close again.

The music stopped as Julia remonstrated with the boys. Helena stared critically at Freya.

'Open your eyes' she commanded as she gently tilted Freya.

Freya's eyes opened and she repeated, 'Hello, hello!'

'Hello' replied Helena calmly.

'You can hear me?' asked Freya.

'Yes,' said Helena 'but you're very quiet'.

Freya was alive with excitement and frustration. She couldn't shout any louder. 'Hold me, to your ear' she said. Helena nestled the fairy into her shoulder. Freya was ecstatic, her soft words drifted into Helena's ear, 'Help me.'

'How can I help you?' replied Helena in her matter-of-fact way.

'The boys get the tree all wrong, every year. It's heartbreaking to sit up there, looking down at it all.'

Helena frowned; she had not thought there was a wrong way to decorate a tree.

'What do you mean?'

Freya sighed, 'It ends up a mess, as if they have thrown everything at the tree and hung it where it has landed.'

When she thought about it, Helena had to agree. The boys were always eager to help with anything, for the first ten minutes. Then they couldn't wait to get the job done and tuck into biscuits.

Freya went on, 'I can tell you and you can tell them where to put things. Together we could make the perfect Christmas tree.'

'Yes, I can do that' whispered Helena.

Julia marshalled the subdued boys back downstairs and explained that the children would each take it in turns to hang a decoration and that Helena could go first. Before that, they had to untangle the lights and put them on the tree. The boys groaned.

'No lights, no Christmas biscuits!' said Julia. Leo picked up the bundle of wire and bulbs and began to unravel it.   After a bit of tugging and minor argument the lights were sparkling as they spiralled around the tree.

'We could change the tradition. You can put Freya Fairy on top first if you like.' said Julia as she turned to Helena.

'Oh no that won't do.' said Freya.

'No, that won't do,' repeated Helena

'I want to tell everyone where to put things.' she said indignantly.

Julia paused for a moment. Helena was showing early signs of fulfilling the prophecy 'though she be little she is fierce' but Julia had never known Helena to be quite so emphatic.

'Well, that is a change from tradition.   Are you sure Helena?'

Helena nodded, and turned her face away as she flashed a triumphant smile that lit her eyes.

It's going to be the best tree ever!' she whispered to Freya.

Londo grabbed the Tin Soldier and Darth Vader together.

'I want these first. A sword and a sabre, they can fight'

'Fight fight!' chanted Leo.

Julia looked quizzically at Helena, who appeared to be straining to hear something.

'Tin Soldier and I arrived together,' said a disappointed Freya.

Helena took a deep breath as she prepared to square up to her brothers and impose her command on the proceedings.

'No. No fighting, the tin soldier and Freya Fairy have been together for always, the Tin Soldier goes near the top'.

Once again Julia looked at the new Helena emerging from under the cloud of her brothers. Julia was puzzled at how her daughter seemed to be aware of the significance of Freya Fairy and the Tin Soldier.

Impatiently Londo marched up to the tree and hung Darth Vader on the tip of a lower branch. Leo quickly hung Obi-Wan on the same branch.

'It's not balanced.' hushed Freya.

'It's not balanced!' barked Helena.

This time Julia was shocked by Helena's newly acquired aesthetic eye.

'Put Obi-Wan at the same height, on the other side' instructed Helena. Leo immediately followed her directions. Everyone was becoming a little surprised at what appeared to be unfolding before them. An opinionated young upstart crow.

Initially they were a little uneasy with this new Bossy Helena. Over the next hour Helena selected and rejected which decorations would make it onto the tree. The flight of angels was in, and the Disney characters were out. The hand-crafted glass woodland animals made the cut, but Julia's Freida Kahlo's did not. Neither did the 'elves on the shelf' or the strings of red beads.

With their sister directing operations the boys got into a rhythm and Julia watched, surplus to requirements as her children took over this family ritual. She reflected as she remembered one Christmas telling her mother to 'go away, I want to do it all'. Now, Julia appreciated how that particular moment must have hurt her mother. The first break that threatened the bond between mother and child. As Julia looked on, she finally appreciated how her mother had always strived to make sure that however far the link between them was stretched, it would never break. Julia was a teenager then, but it all felt too soon for Helena to be pulling away.

Julia was lost in her thoughts when Helena tugged at her jumper. 'Mummy, mummy. I think you should put the Tin Soldier on the tree.'

'Just below me.' said Freya

'Just below Freya Fairy,' said Helena.

Helena stood back as she handed her mother the Tin Soldier. The boys sat quietly at the foot of the tree as Julia stepped forward and hung up the Tin Soldier. She turned to Helena,

'Time for you to put Freya on top of the tree now.' and she bent down to lift Helena up.

Helena whispered to Freya 'I think I might drop you.' Freya looked at Julia and said to Helena, 'Maybe Julia could lift me to the top of the tree one last time.'

Helena was not sure she completely understood but she turned to Julia and held Freya out to her,

'No, you put Freya at the top of the tree one last time.'

'I thought *you* were going to hang Freya Fairy.' replied Julia.

'It's not my turn yet.' said Helena.

The maturity in her young daughter's voice surprised Julia. She knew that children found their own voice, in their own time, but Helena seemed so young to be sounding so grown up.

Julia stood and looked at the tree, with its perfect symmetry of colour, and graduated size of carefully chosen decorations.

'I think it is the most beautiful tree I have ever seen.' said Julia

'So do I,' said Leo.

'Biscuits!' shouted Londo. A quiet voice floated above the sounds of joy and laughter, 'Merry Christmas Helena!'

Julia turned to see Helena blow a kiss towards the tree as she said,

'Merry Christmas Freya'.

ANNABELL'S LETTER TO SANTA

Avril J Evitts

Dear Santa

Do you know I will not be at my house on Christmas. We are going to Disney World. Do you deliver to The Swan hotel? I don't know our room number yet.

I would like a Disney Villains T Shirt, not pink.

Where do you go for your holidays? I thought I saw you when we went on holiday in the summer. I am sure it was you. Dad told me not to point, it wasn't you. I knew it was you. First off I thought it was the fat man from the bakers who everyone says he eats all the profits, and he must eat them for breakfasts because I've never ever seen any profits in the shop. But he is grumpy and you were funny. Specially when you fell in the pool holding a drink. Your head went right under but you kept your arm up and you didn't spill any. A lady said you'd had too many sherbets. I had too many sherbets at Lizzies party because nobody liked them and everyone had one in their party bags so I ate them all. They give you brain freeze they don't make you fall over.
With love from Annabell.

Christmas Crackers – Marcia White

A WINTER BREAK

Nadya Henwood

We took a trip to Iceland
In quest of the Northern Lights,
To celebrate our Christmas
And see some famous sights.

I am not keen on the cold,
But much to my bleak dismay,
His Christmas wish was to go –
A Winter break, anyway!

The land lived up to its name.
Vistas glorious to behold,
A white blanket of snow and ice.
Thermals worth their weight in gold!

Then the Aurora beckoned.
We set out in dead of night
To hunt those elusive lights,
Snug in our coats, done up tight.

We sought them out everywhere
But all the clouds were too low;
They were too obscured that night.
We'd try again tomorrow.

The second night was clearer.
The guide said, "Look there they are!"
"Where?!" – I could only see clouds,
"Just look through your camera!"

"You see the green through the lens,
The naked eye sees all white.
The clouds must be fewer
To behold the perfect sight."

"You mean I've come all this way
Freezing my butt off at night,
To see the lights on a screen!
I could do that at home - right?"

Back in the van we all got,
To search for some clearer skies.
We went up a snowy hill,
No! Not snow, a sheet of ice!

Back down the hill, the van slid,
Lost control, into a ditch.
We were stranded in the dark,
We had to walk – life's a bitch.

We slipped and slid on that ice.
All too soon, we came undone,
Holding hands tight, as we fell
Like dominoes, one by one.

A fractured wrist, the result.
Not the 'break' I had in mind!
Next time, I choose Winter sun,
So I relax and unwind!

Charge of the Light Brigade – Marcia White

KIDNAPPED AT CHRISTMAS (PART ONE)

Sue Shattock

It was very dark. Jingle rolled his shiny coat along the bottom of the container. It was rough and unyielding with a faint whiff of Sellotape. "I think it's a cardboard box. We're trapped in box, that's all, nothing to worry about!" Jingle was always so unbearably positive, of course it was part of his charm but in situations like this, both Ding and Dong were in agreement. To be abducted by the notorious Chimer family this close to Christmas was very worrying, very worrying indeed. They needed an escape plan and needed to come up with something quick.

Fred checked his appearance in the mirror outside the entrance to the Sounds Christmas Party and straightened his Dicky Bow. It had been nice to get an invite from his old employer. Creating the sounds of coincidence as a celestial sound engineer had always been his dream job. He was gutted when he had been made redundant. But of course, every cloud has a silver lining and without experiencing the highs and lows of self-employment he would never have met the gorgeous Miss Grainger. But that's another story that we haven't got time to tell here.

"Well! Here goes nothing".   Fred took a deep breath and pushed open the familiar doors that would lead him into the hubbub of the life he had left behind. He anticipated the welcoming faces and an orgy of festive fare. At least Walter would be there, and he was looking forward to catching up with his best mate to swap adventures.

But the room was empty. True it was full of sounds, but there were no festive trimmings, no clink of glasses or even a tinkle of laughter. No, something was wrong, very wrong. There was the sound of murmuring and groaning, of rustling and clicking. The noises seemed to be centered around the central desk - his old desk to be exact. And as he drew closer, he could see people on the floor, some colleagues that he recognized and some strangers.   They seemed to be searching for something and were oblivious to everything else.

He crept closer. "What on earth is going on?" he whispered, more to himself than to anyone else, but he must have spoken louder than he thought. The searchers froze and turned to him, one of the faces was very familiar to him. "Walter, Walter, what's wrong, you look like you've seen a ghost?" "Oh Fred, thank God you've come. We've lost the recording of the Christmas bells!"

The engineers sat surrounding the console watching Fred's every move.   He was well practiced and was surprised at the ease with which he remembered all the files, the collections and the numerous buttons and lever combinations required to skim the back catalogue. "I can't understand it, it doesn't make any sense. There were three backups, I'm sure there were three. I remember filing them and signing them off just before I left!" He scrolled back the menus scrutinizing the scrambled data. " You're positive the access codes haven't been changed?" Walter shook his head and re-checked the maintenance log. "No, it's down here with a January job number". Fred scratched his head in bewilderment and started crunching the numbers from the beginning and although it was difficult to believe, he was beginning to suspect that the mysterious disappearance of the precious Christmas bell file was no accident.

There was a deep dark silence in the sealed cardboard box. Even Jingle had run out of uplifting things to say. They knew it was just past eleven o'clock on Christmas Eve because the Chimers were sticklers for punctuality and enjoyed taunting their captives with their monotonous tones and strident striking. In defiant reply the captives protested in the only way they knew how. Ding dinged, Dong donged, and jingle, jingled. Little Tinkle and young Ling-a-ling were worryingly quiet, and the elder bells cradled round the little ones to try and provide some comfort.

"What's going to happen to Christmas?" Little Tinkle wailed to Ding and Dong. "How will there be any 'Ding dong merrily on high' without you two? How will it be fun to ride on 'a one-horse open sleigh' without Jingle? It's not right!" Ling-a-ling snuggled closer to the elder bells, she was missing her beloved Ding-a so much, they had never been parted before and she always relied on him to take the lead. "There is nothing to worry about in regard to Christmas," said Dong reassuringly. "It will all be fine, don't you remember, we were asked to do that sound file for this year so we could have a bit of a break". We couldn't be expected to ring through the entire Jubilee and those weeks of Olympic celebrations without a decent break. 2012 has been an exceptional year and thank goodness the sound department were so very forward thinking and created that back up, just in case. So, you see Christmas will go on. No, what we have to worry about is what the Chimers are up to and why they want to keep us in a box. That's the question." "Quite right" echoed Ding. "That is the question".

Belle's Baubles had a shop window that shone with Christmas cheer. Fred remembered the happy times he had spent with Belle and the family the previous year. Somehow it had never felt like work, creating the backup bell file had been a fun assignment, and he had got to know them all very well. So, it made sense that if anyone was to ask the family a favour, it was Fred. The front door was ajar. He pushed at it gently, slightly surprised that there was no Ding-a-ling-a-ling springing to welcome him.   In fact, the whole shop was unexpectedly quiet. "Hello? Is anyone about?" Still nothing. It was all most peculiar.

A glinting winking, teeny tiny light in the middle of the room caught Fred's attention. There was a large pile of green and gold fabric and ... there it was again. A glint that came from underneath the material. He crept a little closer. It was shocking, it wasn't a pile of material at all, it was Belle and Ding-a. He felt for her pulse and to his relief found it was beating hard and loud.

"Wake up Belle, please wake up" he stroked the matted hair away from her strong and perfect features.   "What happened Ding-a and where's Ling-a-ling and the others?" There was a groan, thank heavens she was coming to. "They took them," Ding-a whispered in his little whiny voice. He sounded odd without his constant companion to back him up. "The Chimers just barged in; we didn't have time to do anything. It happened so fast. I just hid, left Ling-a-ling and the others......oh I'm such a coward".

"Don't upset yourself, little one, there was nothing you could have done." Belle stretched her fingers and toes tentatively. "It doesn't feel like I've got any lasting damage. No, this was a very organised raid. It's been coming a long time. Those Chimers have always been jealous of our celebrity status. It's not enough for them to have every hour on the hour, now they want everything, even Christmas!"

Belle groaned as she struggled to become vertical. "Jealousy, that's the problem, it's always been the problem" she continued, "But this time they've gone too far. I don't know why you're here Fred but thank God you are. Go after them, please save them. They're all I've got left in the world."

Fred was about to tell her about the lost recordings, when it occurred to him that this was too much of a coincidence, the recordings and the originals all disappearing on the same night! On Christmas Eve with just an hour to go to their most important performance of the year. "Do you have any idea where they might have been taken?" Fred pressed Belle urgently. "No, I'm sorry..." "I do, I do!" Ding-a hopped from side to side excitedly. "They said something about going back to headquarters - to see Big Ben".

TO BE CONTINUED...

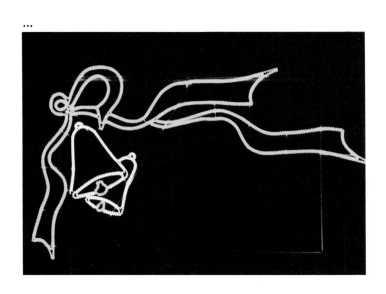

Ding Dong – Marcia White

THE TWELVE DAYS OF CHRISTMAS

Ken Hawkins

On the first day of Christmas my true love gave
to me
'An Amazon wish list',

On the second day of Christmas my true love gave
to me
'A longer Amazon wish list',

On the third day of Christmas my true love gave
to me a note
'Mum's staying for Christmas',

On the fourth day of Christmas my true love gave
to me
'Two bottles of Whiskey',

On the fifth day of Christmas my true love gave
to me a note
'And New Year',

On the sixth day of Christmas my true love gave
to me
'Three bottles of Brandy',

On the seventh day of Christmas my true love
gave to me a note
'Decs are in the loft',

On the eighth day of Christmas my true love gave
to me
'Three hours in casualty',

On the ninth day of Christmas my true love gave
to me
'A pair of crutches',

On the tenth day of Christmas my true love gave
to me
'A foot stool',

On the eleventh day of Christmas my true love
gave to me
'Turkey and pudding'

On the twelfth day of Christmas my true love gave
to me
'A credit card statement – how much'?!

FATHER'S CHRISTMAS

Avril J Evitts

I asked my father what Christmas was like when he was a boy. He told me of his most memorable childhood Christmas, when he was desperate to reach his family in Wales. It is a story of courage, enterprise and endurance.

In the early 1940s, families were uprooted and separated. In January 1941 my father, aged 11, was evacuated with his school from Kingston to the Lake District. His mother took his younger sister and two brothers back to her home in Cwmaman in 'the Valleys' in Wales. They bunked down with their cousins, went to the village school, and spent much of their time picking over the slag heaps for 'nobs', (tiny pieces of coal suitable for starting a fire or using in a potbellied stove). With seven cousins in one household, there was often a bucket of nobs going spare, any surplus was traded with neighbours, the epitome of the 'black market'. There were two shifts in the pit. Four times a day the village cobbles echoed with the march of hob nail boots as the miners made their way to the pithead and back. It was quite common to see a column of coal-black weary men followed by a trail of grubby, happy children, as the miners dropped larger lumps of coal from their pockets for the children to find.

Food was rationed, but many people kept pigs and chickens, and my father's siblings ate well. During the summer they roamed the mountains and Brecon Beacons, collecting bits of wool caught in thistles or on wire fences. Their great grandmother spun the wool, and my aunt was taught how to knit socks and hats for soldiers far from home.

On their first Christmas in Wales, they were given toys made from scraps of wood and fabric. Made by skilled hands, they were robust and included Billy carts, dolls houses, forts with hand carved soldiers and rag dolls with patchwork dresses. Households pooled their ration coupons. Some made Christmas cakes, others Christmas puddings. My grandmother wrote to my father telling him how half the street had crowded into Aunt Megan's. Twenty-two of them had sat down to Christmas dinner, all bringing something for the table, which groaned with meats and treats.

My father's Christmas was a little different. He was billeted with a caring, middle-aged couple. They made the best they could of things at Christmas. My father remembers being given a ruler, a pencil and a notebook, and having a thick slice of ham and vegetables for Christmas dinner.

He missed his family, and as Christmas 1942 approached, he wrote to his mother and told her we would be joining them for Christmas.

My father was 12, and in the pitch-dark early hours of the 22nd of December he set off for Carlisle station where he found the London trains were being re-routed to carry troops to Oxford. He was told if he waited until the afternoon there may be a London train, but it was unlikely he would get a connection to Cardiff. Nothing was going to deter my father from his objective. He was tall and looked older than his years. He had no trouble mingling amongst the soldiers and four hours later he was in Oxford. He enquired about trains to Cheltenham, where he knew he could get a connection to Cardiff. Again, he was a victim of the rescheduling, and no one was quite sure when the next train to Cheltenham was. Speaking to the soldiers he got a lift in an army lorry to Cheltenham. It was a cold, wet day and my father was squeezed into the footwell beside the driver, where they hoped he may be a bit warmer. En route my father told the driver that he was trying to get to Wales, but he wasn't sure if had enough money to get him all the way. News spread of the boy who wanted to get home for Christmas, and a whip round amongst the soldiers gave him the train fare from Cheltenham to Aberdare, 2/3, about 11.5 pence in today's money.

My father eventually arrived in Cardiff at 8pm. He had been travelling for 15 hours and not eaten anything. He was tired, cold, very hungry, and he had missed the last train to Aberdare. Exhausted, my father started to ask the few people milling about if any of them knew how he could get to Cwmaman. An old man said he was catching the train to Merthyr and walking to Aberdare, if my father wanted to join him. Father had a choice; he could wait until morning for the first train or walk with the old man. He decided to press on. When the two unlikely travellers found themselves in Merthyr the train was met by a post office van that was taking parcels to various towns and villages, including Cwmaman. The postman gave the two weary travellers a lift. My father was dropped off at the bottom of the steep road that led up to the Pit Head and he walked the last mile through the dark and silent village. He arrived at midnight, soaked to the skin. Hiis mother stripped off his wet clothes and wrapped him in a rough blanket and gave him a hot drink. She hung his clothes by the fire, where they steamed and hissed as they dried. When he told his mother about his journey and the ride in the post van, she said,

'That's good, you've met Rhys the post. You better get some sleep because you'll be working with him at 6am tomorrow'. My grandmother had arranged for my father to work two 12-hour days helping with the Christmas deliveries.

His grandmother woke Father at 5am with a cooked breakfast and he set off in the first snowfall of the winter. Sure enough, Rhys the Post was waiting for him and explained that Father would be pushing the huge wicker post basket as they delivered to the village and up to the top of Mountain Ash. The postman was laden with three sacks of post and together they made their way through the deteriorating conditions. As they took a short cut over the mountain, the post basket slid on the snow and out tumbled a pile of parcels. Many in brown paper tied with string, some sealed with wax. But there was also an assortment of dead chickens, pheasants and pigeons, with brown labels tied to their feet. My father recalled how he sat on an icy stump, trying to sort everything into some kind of order for delivery. There was a pheasant with no label, and no label could be found.

Rhys looked at my father and said, 'Mrs Rhys wouldn't have a clue what to do with that, you take it boy'. My father did. His mother prepared it for the Christmas table, but my father cannot remember eating any. He was so tired, he spent most of Christmas day asleep.

I found it hard to believe that a 12-year-old boy had such an experience, but his siblings all remembered my father being with them that Christmas and hearing about his adventurous journey. He'd travelled three hundred miles, in the cold light of day and the blackened-out streets at night to have his childhood Christmas in Wales with his family. He did not see them again until September 1945 when they returned to their London home.

WHEN RUDOLPH WENT TO SAINSBURY'S

Sue Shattock

When Rudolph went to Sainsbury's
He wasn't there for sprouts
He bypassed all the broccoli
And the mince pie tasting touts.

He hurried past the best before
Head down, incognito in the crowd
When someone shouted
It's Rudolph! And shouted it quite loud.

It was embarrassing, he felt a fraud
Just looked like his namesake
Yes, his nose was red, he had the flu!
Was he so easy to mistake?

Well, it seems reindeers all look much the same
Until you know them well
Or they're famous faced celebrities
And wear the hallowed Christmas bell.

Sometimes he 'd wished that he was famous
But not now when he felt cr*p
He just wanted paracetamol
And to go straight home for a nap.

And that's typical, you make wishes
And if they do come true
They happen unexpectedly
When you're feeling rough with flu.

All around him shoppers stared and pointed
Made rude remarks about his dripping nose
Tried to touch him and take photos
As he clip-clopped down the rows

He hurried onward to the aisle
Packed with tissues and Lemsip
Found ointment for his bright red nose
And bought night nurse for some kip.

But when he tried to exit,
A crowd of people blocked his way
They wanted selfies with a 'star'
To Instagram on Christmas Day!

It was all too much!
He lost it, then he shouted,
"I'm not the Rudolph that you seek!
You've mistaken me for someone else
He's mostly golden, I'm dark chestnut teak!

I don't even look like stupid Rudolph!
For a start I'm British born and bred
His "people" come from Lapland
I've got a herd in Birkenhead.

I don't jingle, fly or pull a sleigh.
I spend Christmas on my own,
And struggle just to pay the bills.
I don't even own a phone!

So just bog off and leave me be
I'm not famous, not at all
I've just got antlers, feel unwell
And I self-identify as Paul!"

The crowd dispersed quite quickly
Muttering "I reckon Rudolph's had a few"
And the reindeer sadly trudged on homeward
With all his remedies for flu.

A young woman softly said "Excuse me"
Her slight frame was wheelchair bound
She smiled up, her brown eyes blinking
As snow fell gently all around.

"I'm sorry - most people do not mean it
It's partly stupid ignorance
They know little about reindeer
Or what causes them offence.

39

To some, every Reindeer's Rudolph
Every Father Christmas is the one
Every letter gets to Santa
And that lots of snow is always fun!

It sucks to be alone at Christmas
Without friends – it feels so wrong
And to top it all you get abuse and told
"Go back where you belong!"

It's tragic, but if you want to and feel better
Will you join us Christmas Day for tea?
My Mum makes special carrot cake
And we sing carols round the tree!

We'd really love to have you
And hear about your life
It's not easy being different
I know… I'm straight, live in Brighton born in Fife.

And I don't care what colour brown you are
If your nostrils splay too wide
It is the festive season
And we're all flesh and blood inside."

They chatted for a good long while
She completely understood his plight
It only took a few kindly words
To fill his soul with light.

She smiled and left it up to him
And wheeled off on her way
He thought... some people are extra-ordinary
What an unexpected day.

Well, Rudolph was so grateful for the invite
It was his best Christmas wish come true
And this year he'd be less lonely
All because of simple kindness and the flu!

So, remember at this festive time
When you spot deer souls in need
Perhaps take just a moment, understand
And you'll be most blessed indeed.

Snap Crackle and Pop – Marcia White

NADYA'S FESTIVE CODEWORD PUZZLE

Codewords are crosswords with no clues.

Instead, every letter of the alphabet has been replaced by a number, the same number representing the same letter throughout the puzzle.

All you do is **decide which letter is represented by which number**!

To start you off, we have revealed the codes for three letters of the Codeword on the next page.

1	7	15	7	10	25	21	17	13	23	14	9	
4				7						21		
25	21	26	26	15	7	11		8		17 **T**	23 **O**	3 **Y**
13		21		15		21	13	25		13		
9		6				17		7	15	2	7	9
17	16	13	14	22	15	7		9		13		21
6		15		13				7		17	13	14
21		3	23	14		5		14		3		17
9				19	25	23	17	17	23			21
	10	23	16	9		3		9		14		
	23		13			23				23		
7	18	7	9		12	20	13	24	24	7	9	
			4			9				15		

1	2	3 **Y**	4	5	6	7	8	9	10	11	12	13
14	15	16	17 **T**	18	19	20	21	22	23 **O**	24	25	26

44

GONE BUT NOT FORGOTTEN

Sue Shattock

I wrote it down, I know I did,
It was in the middle of last night,
But can I find the blasted thing?
No. It's disappeared from sight.

I think I scribbled on scrap paper
And now I feel a total twit,
It was a pure stroke of inspiration
And the best Christmas poem ever writ!

I've sifted through my papers
And soul searched throughout my brain,
And I can't find any sign of it,
The loss is driving me insane!

This might be it! Oh… illegible,
Well, that's just my luck to date.
I'll have to hope it drifts back in,
No, I won't get in a state.

I should have learned my lesson,
Placed pen and paper by the bed,
But I got caught up wrapping presents,
And then watched Netflix late instead.

I must accept the poem's lost,
That my thought train's been derailed,
It was choc-filled with potential!
But that ship has sadly sailed.

Will just have to wait till next time,
It seems pointless now to moan.
What's done is done, I can't wind back,
Ah... It's Christmas. Can I have a dicta-phone?

JUST DESSERTS

Avril J Evitts

On this day, of all days, I was determined that I would not give my friends a reason to criticise my attempts to become a domestic goddess. My failure to come anywhere near the benchmark was legendary.

A couple of months ago, Monique had declared she was throwing a 'Twixmas' party on December 28th. Judith and Lauren gushed like a burst water main,

'Oh, Monique, you've simply got to let us help.'

Before I could stop myself, I had said, 'I will do the desserts Monique; you can cross those off your list straight away.' This was followed by stunned silence as the girls turned and stared open mouthed. Finally, in unison, they said, 'You'?!

'Of course, me, I CAN cook' issued my traitorous mouth.

'Umm, thank you ... I think', Monique cautiously replied. As I left, I heard Judith's hushed tones, 'She'll never make it herself; I'll bring a batch of my shortcrust mince pies and bite size Christmas Pudding truffles'.

At last, I had the opportunity to prove that I too had read and digested Delia Smith, Jamie Oliver, Gordon Ramsay et al. On the cover of the supermarket December magazine was a picture of a large meringue wreath. The delicate white rim was studded with red and green glace cherries and angelica leaves. Resting on a bed of thick cream the centre was piled high with chopped nuts and fresh berries. After three days, ten dozen eggs and several failed attempts, I finally managed to produce one huge meringue nest. I sat down with a cup of coffee and read the recipe once again.

I had everything I needed with the exception of 'fresh mixed berries'. I was determined this special dessert would eclipse anything my culinary friends had produced, and I headed off into town in search of the freshest of fresh fruits.

An hour and three supermarkets later all I could find was a miserable punnet of tasteless foreign strawberries. I was not going to shy at the first hurdle, and I drove out to the farm shop which I was certain would stock what I wanted.

It did not. I called for the supervisor, who very politely explained that at this time of year they could not offer such a range of soft fruits. Her only suggestion was that I could try the frozen section. In wild indignation I said,

'I shall go elsewhere'.

Ten minutes later I was going around the gyratory system for the third time wondering just where else I was going to go. Time was slipping away. Extreme circumstances call for desperate measures, and in defeat I drove to Iceland, where I found mixed berries, albeit in the form of frozen blocks of indeterminate origin. I laid the frozen bags out on the floor in the car and put the heater on full blast.

By 4pm every surface in the kitchen was covered with bowls of whipped cream. Like a chemist hot on the trail of some major discovery I ran between the bowls, stirring furiously as I added sugar, vanilla and a nip (or two, Ok three) of rum. I was at last ready to assemble my Christmas Wreath. I tentatively eased the meringue onto a large tray. Cracks radiated from the centre, threatening total collapse. I branded every celebrity chef a traitor and screamed in despair. Then the words of my old domestic science teacher echoed across time.

'All you really need to know is how to make the perfect white sauce and how to whip double cream. One will cover up savoury disasters, the other will take care of collapsed desserts'. I carefully pasted the pieces together. Like freshly fallen snow on a muddy field, all imperfections were hidden under a perfectly smooth gleaming white blanket.

The fruit had leaked into the carrier bags and far from being an appetising exotic cocktail, it now resembled the mush that is laughingly referred to as 'fruit' in corner yoghurts. The whole effect was not sumptuous plump berries on top of billowing clouds, rather it resembled the grubby stained bird droppings that can be seen in the early autumn when the birds have been gorging on blackberries.

It was too late now; I drove as fast as I dared and pulled up to find the lights were low, the music was high, there was plenty of party atmosphere. With free-flowing vino there was a chance no one would be able to actually see what they were eating. I jammed the tray against the door frame and rang the bell. As Monique flung open the door, the whole lot fell in a heap on the welcome mat, along with all my hopes and dreams of becoming a member of the not-so-secret society of super women. Amid unrestrained laughter Monique declared at stadium volume, 'Anna you are a hoot'.

A hoot! I had not trawled half the county on literally a fruitless search, spent hours in the kitchen and put myself through a nervous breakdown for a hoot!

'But I ...'

'I didn't think you were serious darling' giggled Monique, 'We went shopping this morning'. She waved her hand in the direction of the dining room, where a delicious display of frozen desserts was arranged around the piece de la resistance, Mary Berry's Christmas Wreath Pavlova.

SEAN'S LETTER TO SANTA

Avril J Evitts

Dear Santa,

How are you?

I hope you are well.

I am well.

I would like a Batmobile for Christmas. The one with flashing lights, and the wings that flip out when you press the button. And it's the one with Batman in his cape, but not the one with the cloth cape because that looks silly. The one that fires bullets out of the front and it has a rocket up its back.

I don't like Robin, so not the one with Batman and Robin together. Not the lego Batmobile because I haven't got time to build it AND play with it. And anyway you can't actually play with the lego one because as soon as you pick it up and start flying it about all the bits fall off and then my Dad treads on the lego bits on the carpet and he swears something terrible.

I hope you have the right one, there are lots of different Batmobiles. If you are not sure, it will be the one that is the most expensive. I know because Dad says I always want what costs the most money.

Love from Sean

PS If you are out of stock, they have the one I want in Smiths Toys at Quayside. On the middle shelf, not the one on the bottom shelf. Dex has got that one and I don't want to be a copycat.

Naughty or Nice? – Marcia White

A CHRISTMAS CANCELLATION

Sue Shattock

This morning my mother tested positive
I saw her yesterday
Now our Christmas has been cancelled
And her birthday's on boxing day....

93 years young!

I'm eating Christmas lunch alone
In case I get the bug
She thought she had a little cold
And I gave her comfort in a hug

So...

The table's set, the presents wrapped
I lit the festive candle just for me
I've cancelled get-togethers
And there's no "just popping out for tea"

My mother's strong and coping
My sister's masked up, going round
I'll just have to wait till Wednesday
To see if dear Omicron is found

It's a mistake to think it's over
That "It's just a heavy cold,
I'm not testing, I'll just gargle"
No! It's still a present danger for the old

So, when in doubt please stay at home
And keep those germs at bay
Our Christmas has been cancelled
Well, postponed till New Years Day.

Spirals in the night – Marcia White

PHONE A FRIEND AT CHRISTMAS

Sue Shattock

Hello…?   Hello, it's Omicron,
Yes, I know it's 3am!
In case you're worried, I'm okay,
Have you forgotten me again?

I'm feeling flat and rather down,
Quite abandoned and alone…
No! I'm not just seeking sympathy
I had no one else to phone.

I admit, I've been a bit diluted lately,
By that British vaccine plot!
But I still get 'searched' on social media
And I trend on Instagram a lot.

But I'm feeling very 'off the boil',
Can't get into festive gear,
Hello…?   Are you still listening?
It's very hard to hear…

Yes… yes. Perhaps I need to take a course?
That new Paul McKenna one would do,
I'm lacking inner confidence,
And could lose a pound or two.

I'm not sure where it all went wrong,
I rather liked my reign
As a virtual viral Santa Claus,
Spreading gifts, immersed in fame.

I suppose I could have done it differently,
Yes… It could be a 'blip', or viral block.
I appreciate your wise advice,
Happy Christmas, speaking clock.

It's nice to know that at least time is on my side!

FIRST CHRISTMAS DOWN UNDER

Ken Hawkins

The rain had stopped - the rain that had greeted us when we arrived. We stood in a tin dockside shed, it may not have been called a shed but at the age of eleven, a tin roofed, tin sided building was a shed. The rain made it feel cold - a damp cold. The cold was different here, it had a smell of damp socks.

The shed was full of people who had just disembarked from a ship, an emigrant ship. After its epic voyage it was disgorging more ten-pound poms. The people queued with their bags to be inspected by what looked like soldiers with the word 'Customs' on their jacket sleeve. These customs men were looking at our cases and bags. They found the fact that I was carrying a cricket bat of particular interest. The one who was talking to me decided to use my bat to pretend to be batting an invisible ball. He remarked, 'Was I here for the test?'. Which I thought was strange as the last test I did was the eleven plus. He gave the bat back and I joined the rest of the family – mum and dad and my two sisters - and we left the shed.

When we left, my uncle was waiting with the car. We squeezed in but there was not enough room for all the luggage and people, so a taxi was hired. The journey to my aunt's and uncle's house took about half an hour. I was fascinated by the Melbourne trams and how the cars negotiated them. We pulled up outside a large red building that was in fact another tin shed, although this did have windows and a door which made it a house. It was surrounded by trees and bushes that flapped in the wind and rain. Inside the house, the rain bouncing off the roof made the sound of a drum - a very loud drum.

The tiredness of making such a long journey was beginning to become intense; I fell asleep in a chair still clutching my cricket bat. I suddenly awoke with a strange noise in my head, it was a type of tapping. At first, I thought it was more rain, but it was harder than rain like something running across the roof. I listened a little longer, had no idea what it could be, then a voice from the kitchen announced, 'possum on the roof again!'. 'What's a possum?' I asked. Sufficiently assured that this creature was not a threat I fell asleep again.

What I thought was all night was in fact barely half an hour. As my eyes focussed, I saw it, large with legs that appeared to go on forever. It just looked down at me, but of course it was looking at the other end of the ceiling. It didn't move, it just looked and looked, but spiders this big just stayed and waited – my first meeting with a Huntsman – it would not be my last. They were large and ugly but harmless, but their much smaller cousins were another story. I was to confront them later. My uncle confirmed that they were harmless, and they ate lots of smaller insects. This information did not fill me with confidence. I was certain it had me on the menu. I was regaining my confidence and hoping to fall asleep, when a scream punctured the evening.

The harmless spider had moved into the room where my mother was resting. Her reaction and screaming were less measured than mine. To the scream was added 'We're going home!'. Going home? We had only just arrived. The thought of another four weeks at sea, rolling and pitching water crashing about, desperately clutching your plate lest your food is thrown to the floor or should that be the deck? I think that's a no, no. The spider had moved, and the screaming stopped and the immediate bon voyage had been cancelled.

This auspicious introduction to life down under was over. Having arrived in the school winter break I had a couple of weeks freedom before my introduction to being a 'pom', but it didn't last, friends were made whether they be Aussie or German, Italian or a plethora of nationalities. The playground was, and still is, a great leveller. Chasing girls is fun anywhere in the world. As the weeks passed, the temperature began to increase. My birthday that year was a warm Spring day where the previous year it had been an Autumn chill. Christmas was coming and it was getting hotter - a lot hotter - 104F(40C) degrees on Christmas eve followed by 98F (36.6C) on Christmas day and all before global warming. Despite these temperatures, we still had Christmas decorations, and there was a tree which our first Aussie moggy made an energetic attempt to demolish. The mince pies, the cream which was kept in a fridge, a fridge was no longer a luxury but a necessity. Also useful for putting your head in to cool down! A full Christmas dinner was available as normal, but as it was summer, this just added to my confusion. Letters from relatives and the TV news showed that back in Britain they were having the worst winter ever with large snow drifts, in which trains were stuck, schools closed, and farms were cut off.

Oh, how I missed snow at Christmas!

Sunburst – Marcia White

SWEET TREATS

Avril J Evitts

Della leaned on the low wall outside the Village Hall. She was soon joined by other Mums, Dads and Guardians, gathered to collect their little ones from playgroup. With her partner away from Monday to Friday, Della was eager to chat with a grown up and catch up on village news.

Everyone was swapping tips about the upcoming Nativity play. Rendezvous were arranged to swap tea towels, last year's costumes or scraps of material to dress sheep, shepherds and angels. Pamela, whose third child was at the playgroup strode up, 'You know what day it is?'

Everyone looked blank, Della worried that she had forgotten something trivial in the grand scheme of things but vital to her three-year-old's social standing. Sponsorship form? Maybe it was 'bring a bear day'. Della couldn't think what was significant about today.

'Sugar mice' declared Pam as Moira, the Playgroup Leader, opened the double doors. The children were usually struggling into their hats and coats. However today they were seated on the large circular reading rug.

'The children have been making something special this morning. They will come up individually to collect the Christmas gift they have made for you.' announced Moira.

One by one the children were called to collect sugar mice, of various shapes and sizes. They each took their mouse and proudly presented it. Della stared at the grey mouse, complete with a mottled fuzzy coat of dust. She struggled to maintain her best proud-Mum smile as she contemplated the grubby morsel. The children had obviously spent all morning rolling white fondant icing all over the floor.

One mother whispered in horror what they were all thinking, 'I haven't got to eat it have I'?

As Pam's daughter presented her mouse, Pam said loudly, 'I think that's so special we had better save it for Daddy'.

There were sighs of relief all round as deals were struck to save the special mice for special people. Della tried to cajole her son into saving the mouse for grandpa until her son shouted, 'Grandpa hates sweet things' and before she could stop him, her son snatched the mouse and tucked into the grey moulded mass of sugar and sweepings.

'He'll be fine,' chirped Pam, 'They all eat a bucketful of dirt before they're five'.

'Not all in one go though!' laughed Della.

SUGAR MICE

(Makes 12 Mice)

INGREDIENTS:

- 1 EGG WHITE

- 1 TSP LEMON JUICE

- 400-500G SIFTED ICING SUGAR

- PINK FOOD COLOURING

- SMALL CHOCOLATE SPRINKLES.

- KITCHEN STRING ABOUT 48CMS

- COCKTAIL STICK.

- BAKING PAPER OR GREASEPROOF PAPER FROM INSIDE A CEREAL PACKET.

METHOD:

1. Put the egg white in a large bowl and whisk until foamy, add the lemon juice.

2. Gradually stir in the icing sugar until the mixture is really stiff like dough.

3. Divide the mixture in half and add a drop of food colouring to one half.

4. Tip out and knead until the icing is an even pink colour.

5. Break off a walnut sized piece of the mixture and roll into a rounded cone shape.

6. Flatten one side so that the mouse can sit on a flat surface without falling over.

7. Pinch out little ears on the narrow end and then squeeze the same end into the nose.

8. Press chocolate sprinkles below the ears to make two eyes.

9. Cut a piece of string, about 4cm, and push in the rounded end to make a tail.

10. Use a cocktail stick to dab a small amount of pink onto the nose.

Place the sugar mice onto a piece of baking parchment and allow to dry for about 12 hours.

EXCEPT FOR A MOUSE

Avril J Evitts

Twas the night before Christmas, when all
through the house
Not a creature was stirring, except for a mouse.
He tiptoed softly, treading with care
Avoiding the creak, he missed the last stair.

The children slept softly in their own little beds,
As Dreams of sugar mice, danced in their heads.
Mouse put on his coat, and his red woollen cap,
He was cold being woken from a warm winter's
nap.

He tripped over the fire irons, they fell with a
clatter,
He heard someone wake, shout 'what is the
matter'.
He raced up the stairs was gone in a flash,
Into the skirting, to check on his stash.

Through a gap in the brick, he could see the thick
snow
'My whiskers' he shivered, 'it's nine below'.
Then out on the lawn, what should appear,
A white fat cat Santa and eight tiny reindeer.

Mouse hurried outside, down the pipe double
quick,
Cat stroked his false beard, 'Tonight I'm St Nick'.
He grinned at mouse, 'I'm so glad you came'
'Meet my reindeer' and he called them by name!

'Now Dasher! Now, Dancer! Now, Prancer and
Vixen!
Dear, Comet! Dear, Cupid! And Donner and
Blitzen!
Startled, they leapt, they crashed into the wall.
'Push off' shouted Mouse, Dash away all!'

Spurring them on Cat shrieked, 'go faster we'll
fly',
But they fell on their backs and stared at the sky
None could remember if they ever flew.
They were all of a tangle, they hadn't a clue.

A gust of wind lifted them, right up to the roof
They were prancing and pawing with each little
hoof.
They were going in circles around and around,
When down the chimney fell St Nick in a bound.

Dressed in white fur from his head to his foot,
He got covered in ashes and ten years of soot.
Mouse laughed out loudly, 'why cat you're all
black'
'Alice won't like it, you may as well pack'.

Cat sneered, 'there's no need Mouse, to make so
merry
I'm set on cake and you're the cherry!
Cat took out his kerchief and gave a good blow
'You better run mouse, off you go'

Cat chased after mouse and bared his teeth,
He glanced at the tree and found a small wreath.
Cat threw it at mouse, hit his plump little belly,
Poor mouse was shaking his legs turned to jelly!

Down from the tree came a jolly old elf,
'Great shot, Cat, couldn't do better myself!
'But I think I would've aimed for his head',
Mouse was quivering, afraid, full of dread.

Mouse had to think quickly, it might just work,
It relied on Cat being a total jerk
Mouse lurched at Cat and bit his nose,
In a panic Cat jumped; up the chimney he rose!

He sprang to his sleigh, to his team gave a
whistle,
This time they flew, like down from a thistle.
Mouse stood triumphant as they drove out of
sight,
"Happy Christmas fat cat, and to all a good-
night!"

So Relaxing – Marcia White

BRUCE'S LETTER TO SANTA

Avril J Evitts

Dear Santa,

I think I have been good, OK, I haven't been bad.

I would like a trumpet for Christmas.

Santa, I don't think you got our letters. The last two years I asked for a trumpet and my brother Toby asked for a drum kit. I know we don't always get what we want, Mum said it depends how much money you've got. But last year Toby got a new iPad AND a games console; and I got a mountain bike. These must have cost way more than a trumpet.

Mum says it might be because the noise will be too much for the neighbours. When they make screaming noises Dad just knocks on the bedroom wall so all they have to do is bang on the wall and me and Toby will knock it off.

I am posting this letter in the post box to be sure you get it. We never used to set the letters alight to go up the chimney. We used to leave them on the mantlepiece. We only started setting fire to them a couple of years ago when Mum said we were old enough now that we went to Beavers. The whole burning thing doesn't seem to be working. And I'm not sure it is doing Mum's mental health any good because she stands with the watering can in her hand when we light the matches.

I hope you have made enough money at whatever it is you do for the rest of the year to be able to give all the children the things they would like, except for Will in Arndale Avenue. He says he wants an AK47, but Santa, I wouldn't give him a water pistol.

Mum says we have to be kind to Will because he is learning slower and he will soon learn to be a bit more grown up, but she doesn't see Will jumping off the garage roofs or trying to peg his baby sister on the washing line. Will had a cat and it ran away, and Mum says we can't choose a cat 'cos cats choose where they will live. Will's cat definitely didn't want to live with him anymore and there must be a reason for that. Will's Mum was pretty good at feeding the cat. She would give it Will's Dad's sausages if he got home too late. Once she locked him out, not the cat. So defo Santa, don't give Will anything he can shoot.

Love from Bruce

P.S. Mum says Morrisons put out a whole box of carrots for the reindeer, so we don't have to. I hope you like the Gin and tonic and Truffles. Mum told us last week that she read you don't like milk and mince pies anymore.

I'm in the right place! – Marcia White

CHRISTMAS SHOPPING FOR PEACE

Sue Shattock

Can you help...? Can anyone help?

I'm Christmas shopping for peace this fine
morning
But there doesn't seem much good stuff in stock,
I've tried M&S and the Co-op
Sports Direct and that florist right next to the
clock.

I've searched high and low in the high street.
Been to Waitrose and am now resting here,
But there's no sign of any peaceful solutions,
Or ointments or salves in the air.

And still the bombs keep on falling,
The carnage appalling.
More death than we will ever forgive.
And the finger of blame
The hate and the pain
Will haunt generations as long as they live.

I'm Christmas shopping for peace this fine
morning,
It's the one thing on my list not ticked 'done.'

There's been a run on gifts of supplies
Of guns, tanks and knives,
It's all free postage and buy two for one.

I can get a peace candle
And a stay peaceful manual
From 'Smiths' or that 'Between the Lines' place,
But we need concrete and lasting
Not a patchwork of plastering
And it all needs to happen at pace.

I'm Christmas shopping for peace this fine
morning,
Can I order if I pre-pay on my card?
Send to Gaza/Ukraine,
To wherever there's pain?
Why on earth is this search quite so hard?

And still the bombs keep on falling
The carnage appalling,
More death than we will ever forgive.
And the finger of blame
The hate and the pain
Will haunt generations as long as they live.

I'm Christmas shopping for peace this fine
morning
We've run out and it just **will not do**!
The containers are being held back for no reason
In a roadblock that won't let them get through.

I'm Christmas shopping for peace and will find
it!
It's in the hearts of incredible men,
In brave women and children and students,
It's in the stories that emerge from your pen.

I'm Christmas shopping for peace this fine
morning,
And I've been scouring shops so far in vain,
It's all gone on too long. Bloody war is just
wrong!
So, the search must begin once again.

Can you help…? Can anyone help? It's Christmas!

AVRIL'S LONDON LIGHTS QUIZ

1. In which year was the first laser light used in Oxford Street?
    a. 1979
    b. 1978
    c. 1976

2. The Savoy Theatre in London was the first in the world to be entirely lit by incandescent light bulbs. In which year?
    a. 1881
    b. 1890
    c. 1875

3. In which London Street did traders come together to create a   Christmas light display?
    a. Regent Street
    b. Oxford Street
    c. Bond Street

4. In which year did Christmas Lights first appear in London's west end?
    a. 1951
    b. 1959
    c. 1954

5. In 2017 Selfridges' window display included:
    a. 3D printed models of the moon and planets
    b. Paintings by primary school children
    c. 5,000 hand painted Bussell Sprouts

6. When was the first London's New Years Day Parade?
    a. 1987
    b. 1967
    c. 1957

7. When was the first Christmas Tree in Trafalgar Square?
    a. 1946
    b. 1948
    c. 1947

8. How many times has Kylie Minogue switched on lights in London?
    a. Three times
    b. Once
    c. Twice

9. In 1964 Cliff Richard (and The Shadows) appeared in which Pantomime at the London Palladium?
    a. Puss in Boots
    b. Aladdin
    c. Jack and the Beanstalk

10. In 1904 who donated the cup for the Serpentine Swimming Club 's annual Christmas Day swim?
    a. J M Barrie
    b. H G Wells
    c. Edward VIII

ANSWERS ON BACK PAGES

Who lives behind this door? – Marcia White

KIDNAPPED AT CHRISTMAS (PART TWO)

Sue Shattock

The bright light blinded the little band of bells. They were surrounded by muffled laughter and a few giggles. The huge shape of Sir Benjamin Chimer loomed above them. Jingle jingled merrily, partly in defiance but mostly because he didn't know what else to do. "Silence" boomed the huge presence. "You will be silent!". The bells gazed up in terror as the giggles turned to laughter and the laughter into a deep dark menacing sound.

Fred took the first guard by surprise. It was one of the chunky chimes and was easy to overpower. The second and third guards had taken a bit more effort, but since he had started on his training with Miss Grainger, he was getting surprisingly fit. If someone at the Christmas party had asked if he had been working out......well, this year he had!

As he inched nearer to the central chamber he could hear the boom of Sir Benjamin. If he could just get a bit closer.........and get his Digi-recorder going he might discover what was really going on and save his friends. He sighed with relief as the little red recording light blinked on, it was old fashioned kit, but it had never let him down. The time was ticking and there was less than half an hour to Christmas. Exactly twenty-three minutes to save and record the Belles and get back to the office before all was lost. Fred had been in a lot of scrapes before, but this was pushing things to the wire. Christmas was now just minutes away.

"We're going to ruin you, destroy you" boomed Ben. "No one will remember you after you fail to turn up with your magic this Christmas". The Chimers started to applaud their revered leader, nodding their heads in agreement and grunting their approval. Jingle was beginning to get angry now. He rather wished his sister Jangle was around to help. She was always having a go and getting on people's nerves. "You're just trying to frighten us; well it won't work. Shame on you, frightening the little ones" he shouted. Both Ling-a-ling and Tinkle were still hiding behind Ding and Dong but screamed out loud together, "Yes shame on you!" Ding and Dong started Dinging and Donging together and inspired, the others all joined in to create a cacophony of sound and chucked in all the Christmas carols they could muster.

With all the noise, at least Fred now knew where the missing Bells were - at the bottom of that cardboard box surrounded by very angry Chimers holding their hands over their ears. They couldn't bear to hear anything discordant or unexpected and when they stepped away to block out the wall of sound, Fred grabbed his chance. Rewinding his recording machine, he slammed up the recorded sound to full volume. The bells, jingles and the carols blasted out, filling the whole room with bone aching noise. All the Chimers including Big Ben were stunned and disorientated. Staggering around blindly, trying to protect themselves from the terrible chaotic sound that surrounded them. Fred grabbed the box and legged it down the stairs and out into the snowy night.

"Thank you so much, you've saved us" squeaked Jingle, "but can't we go a bit slower we're getting all shaken up!" The Belles were bouncing around in the bottom of the box. "I may have saved you, but now you need to save Christmas! There was now less than four minutes to go, and knowing the Chimers, Fred was afraid that they might try something else underhand to get their way. The bells were certainly getting shinier because of the friction, but they were also feeling rather sick. "We did the tapes, what do you mean? What do you mean save Christmas?" But there was no time for Fred to speak, only to run!

Fred's fear was justified. The midnight Chimes had started early. Walter and his colleagues waited anxiously beside the silent sound console. The countdown had begun and there was no sign of Fred or the missing Bells. The team had bodged together some substitute sounds, got together a few ringtones and doorbells, but they knew it was no substitute and wouldn't fool anyone for long. Further investigation had shown that all three back up tapes of the bells had been wiped and the culprit, a small chiming mantel clock masquerading as a Christmas present had been apprehended trying to escape, disguised as a dud battery. Unfortunately for Malcolm the Chimer, it hadn't been a very convincing or successful disguise because the battery concerned had been a rechargeable one. Belle and Ding-a had arrived just a few minutes earlier and explained the situation - that there was still a chance that Fred would succeed.

Belle was still feeling a bit wobbly. "Well, if he doesn't arrive in time, you'll just have to implement plan B" the team fixed their eyes on Walter's ashen features. The 7th chime had spoken, only 5 to go. "You have got a plan B, haven't you? There's always a plan B!" Walter put his head in his hands and shook it slowly.

On the tenth chime Fred crashed through the door carrying his precious cargo. Belle rushed forward "Oh my darlings, my darlings are you alright?" Walter quickly moved out of the hot seat "If anyone can do this Fred, it's you, you're the bell expert!" Without hesitation, Fred jumped into the vacant console seat, strapped himself in and clamped the waiting earphones over his head. "There's no time, focus!" Heaving and panting, adjusting levers and creating sparks, Fred exploded into action. "We're going live in 5, are you ready? Ding, Dong, Jingle?" The bells had been gently helped out of their box prison by an ecstatic Belle and sat unmoving on the edge of the sound desk looking dazed. "I don't think I can do this, wailed Tinkle, I don't feel well". Fred was concentrating hard on the incoming message folder. The clock struck midnight. "Walter! Man the stations, it's started!". Messages and requests were flooding in thick and fast. But the Bells just sat there, with a glazed expression on their shiny faces. Fred was beginning to despair. "Look guys, I know it's a big ask after all you've been through, but you can't let the Chimers win, you've got to give me something here. Jingle we've got incoming, 27,000 jingles. Ding, Dong we've got bell requests coming in from all over the world. Tinkle we really need to get the baby bells going. Please!" But the bells all just sat there, silent, looking blankly into the far distance.

Ding-a held out his hand to Ling-a ling. "You can do this, we've got to wake them up, now, together Ding-a!" Ling-a-ling looked at him blankly. "You can't have forgotten my darling, just concentrate. Ding-a!" There was no response at all. Nothing. Shaking his head in despair, tears rolling down his cheeks. Ding-a couldn't help wailing, "I've lost her, oh Ling-a-Ling please come back to me, I love you so much".

The shrill sound of the telephone cut through the edgy silence; it was a brief one-sided conversation. Walter shook his head, "Big Ben is laughing, he wants to know if we need any help, do we need any help, Fred?" With all eyes on him, Fred was beginning to doubt. The consoles were now full of unfulfilled orders for Christmas Bells. The screens overloaded with millions of tiny pinpricks, requests from all over the world. Maybe, there was nothing else to do except concede defeat. Unless, unless...it was a long shot, but a long shot was all there was.

"Belle, when I used to visit, we sang that song together, do you remember?" "Yes, the silver bells song!" Fred was thinking fast, "Lets sing the silver bells song; you told me that the silver bells had magic. And to be frank we don't just need a bit of magic; we need a miracle!" Walter had just been dealing with another insistent phone call. This time it was from the boss, and he was now looking anxiously at his watch. "We've only got a few minutes left Fred, then he's going to pull the plug. Apparently, the Chimers are very insistent." "Belle, sing the song, it's our only hope." Fred was working hard to stop the inevitable overload.

Belle's beautiful pure voice hung in the air around them and she began with the chorus:

"Silver Bells, Silver Bells,

Its Christmas time in the city,

Ring-a-ling, hear them ring

Soon it will be Christmas day"

Somehow the sound seemed to dissolve the panic that had previously engulfed them, and in a few moments the whole room had joined in with Belle. Even Walter was humming along, mesmerized by the magic of Belle's soothing tones. Then the miracle slowly started to take shape.

First Ding and Dong began humming softly before being joined by Jingle. Then Tinkle started to awaken and, surrounded by the familiar comforting sound, Ling-a-ling soon stirred in Ding-a's protective arms. She gave a little sigh and snuggled closer. She's coming round, DING-A!" He shouted at the top of his voice. "Ling-a-ling" came the sleepy reply. The response was faint at first, but soon grew to full power "DING-A-LING-A-LING!" The room was suddenly filled with the sound of awakened Bells all wanting to be heard. DING-A-LING-A-LING, DING-A-LING-A-LING! "She's back, they're all back!"

Fred was grinning, "I can hear that! I've always loved those silver bells!" Heaving a sigh of relief and a whooping for joy Fred bounced over to Belle "You're an angel!" Hugging her tightly he twirled her round and round and when they eventually turned to face Ding, Dong, Jingle and the rest, they were all laughing with relief.

"So guys, are you ready to go back to work?!" Even Fred was taken aback by the enthusiastic response. Suddenly the air was filled with the Dings, Dongs and Jingles of excitement. Even Tinkle was back on tip-top sparkling form. "Right then, it's show time" said Fred grinning and sitting himself at the sound console, now groaning and alive with Bell requests, "So, all we have to do *now* is to save Christmas......piece of cake!"

Church Bells – Marcia White

GARETH'S LETTER TO FATHER CHRISTMAS

Avril J Evitts

Dear Father Christmas

I would like a job. When I leave school I want to work in your workshop. I like making things. I made the Blue Peter Tracy Island and my mates thought it was quite good.   If I come and work for you I could be the Tracy Island maker.   I will need these things:

Grocery Box
Cereal pack, cardboard
Newspapers
Kitchen foil
PVA glue
Soap powder packet (1kg size)
Oblong cheese box
Paper bowl
Washing-up liquid bottle
Potato crisp tube
Small sticky labels
Blue and grey pens
75 mm flower pot saucer

93

Sandpaper
2 medium and 1 small matchbox
Sponge
Drinking straw
Corrugated paper
Brass paper fastener
Blue card
Pipe cleaners
Green and brown crepe paper
Green, brown and grey paint
Sawdust

Anthea Turner says everyone has these things in their house. We didn't and Mum said it would have been cheaper to buy a Tracy Island. I have a lot of left over paint and paper and drinking straws I could bring.

I hope to hear from you soon

Yours Gareth, Tracy Island Maker

Full Circle – Marcia White

LOOKING GLASS CIRCLES

Sue Shattock

We go round in looking glass circles,
No sunrise is ever the same,
We go round and around till the sunset,
Then the cycles repeat once again.

My memories keep on turning,
But the Christmas wish-list is the same,
And every year I'm yearning,
Just to see your face again.

I think I glimpse you in the gilded glass,
Whilst hanging baubles on our tree
A memory of a life now past
But it still feels like yesterday to me.

You seem jolly, laughing, smiling,
But can this really be?
I'm not jolly, laughing, smiling.
No!   You didn't stay with me.

You flew away, no backward glance,
Vanished on your sleigh.
Now you're jolly, laughing, smiling.
Why? Did you have to go away?

You were my Santa Claus at Christmas
My Easter bunny in the spring
You brought extra sunshine to my summer,
You were my Autumn everything…

Don't laugh but…

This year I've left your favourite, sherry trifle!
With a coffee and a beer.
Those mint humbugs that you loved so much,
And some carrots for those damned deer.

'Cos I miss you most on Christmas Eve
It was our journey's end.
But I still cycle back to yesterday,
And pause fondly on our bend.

This Christmas…

When I glimpse you in the gilded glass
I'll smile when you see me,
And celebrate a life now past,
And of you standing close to me.

Yes, you're always standing close to me.

We go round in looking glass circles,
But no sunrise is ever the same.
We go round and around till the sunset.
Then the cycles repeat once again.

Once again

Once again

WHO IS FATHER CHRISTMAS
Ken Hawkins

Who is Father Christmas?

The evening was dark, but the excitement was intense. The one evening I looked forward to going to bed. All those letters to the north pole, had they arrived? Would the presents I hoped and wished for really be at the end of my bed or in my stocking? Christmas is wonderful when you're six.

All the previous Christmas joy of dolls and board games. Packets of sweets and a selection box. But now it was sensible stuff, new coats and shoes but there were still some chocolates - dad always saw to that. I knew Father Christmas didn't exist, but I kept the pretense for my younger sister. But you still want to believe even at ten.

A new stereo, the shape of the box gave it away. No need to unwrap the other presents that looked suspiciously like clothes. Why do parents use Christmas to provide children with new clothes? But then there was another one wrapped in plain gold paper tied with a blue ribbon and a bow on top. Who is it from? He still exists in the surprise, the excitement. Christmas still has magic even at twelve.

Hopefully, this year there will be no clothes. But something frivolous, you know a piece of what is really junk, but that will make me laugh. Oh, please no books for uni. Dad would know what I mean. Also, I must buy him something useless, no power tools this year. Christmas needs to be a little practical at eighteen, but not completely.

Christmas this year at home after three years away. All the presents in my case; dropped at the door by the taxi. There is one present even Santa cannot give if he were real, my dad. Christmas can be hard when you're twenty–one and life is so real.

Father Christmas was just my dad. But I always knew that.

OLIVER'S PENGUIN

Nadya Henwood

There once was a penguin named Oliver
Whose aim in life was to be jollier.
The trouble was he did not like the cold,
So he decided to be brave and bold.

Across the seas he travelled far and wide,
Down the depths and up the waves, he would
glide.
He did not know his destination,
Just that warmth was his motivation.

After some time, he grew tired.
He was lost and uninspired.
He felt lonely and wanted his mum,
He was no jollier, he was glum.

Just when he had lost all hope,
Began to sob and to mope,
A girl called Lara swam by,
She stopped when she heard him cry.

What's wrong with you?' she said.
He looked up, eyes all red.
'I swam away from home,
But now I'm all alone!'

'Don't worry, you can come home with me.
I'll look after you, I'm a mummy.'
'But I can't swim anymore!
I'm tired, not like before.'

'You can lie on my back and sleep,
I can swim home, no need to weep.'
So off they went, penguin and mum,
Him snoozing, lying on his tum.

Suddenly, he woke up with a start,
To see two eyes staring at his heart.
'Hello, I'm Oliver.' said the boy.
'You must be my newest Christmas toy.'

'I'm not a toy, I've swum from far away!
And where on earth is this place, anyway?'
'This is sunny Malta, don't you know?'
'Sunny?!' gasped Oliver all aglow.

'But wait, my name's Oliver too.
Are you sure that's what they call you?'
'Of course! Then we're made for each other!
But you know I'm also a brother.'

'Huh?' 'Yes, I have a sister too.
Lucy will want to meet with you.'
'I've always wanted a sister,
But we can't both be Oliver!'

'Then from now on, you can be Ollie,
Because you're a penguin so jolly!'
And so, Ollie's wish had come true,
Sun, sea, and a family too!

CRACKER JACK

Sue Shattock (Inspired by Marcia's pictures)

Small in stature, big of heart,
He paints bright baubles for the tree.
And has a magic paintbrush,
That sets inner starlight free.

It adds jingles into jingle bells,
Gives super twinkle to the light,
Paints extra sparkle into stars,
To make them shine more bright.

Jack's best-known work was long ago
A commission from above.
A star that changed our history,
And filled the world with love.

Its sparkle blazed in daylight,
It beamed out rays of light.
The start of all our Christmas times
On that first great silent night.

Its brightness guided wise men,
Although the way was steep.
It inspired faith and courage,
Lured shepherds from their sheep.

To find the baby in the manger
The miracle of a birth
That called all the world together
With hope for peace on earth.

It made Cracker Jack quite famous,
But he didn't like the fuss.
So grew a very large moustache
And changed his name to Gus.

And to keep himself unrecognised,
He wears uniforms and hats.
Sports stripey socks from M&S
And sells his portraiture of cats!

He prefers a quiet life at Christmas,
Paints bright baubles for the tree.
And with the magic in his paintbrush
Can spread joy and love for free.

Ready to Party? – Marcia White

ALICIA'S LETTER TO FATHER CHRISTMAS

Avril J Evitts

Dear Father Christmas

I don't want a present for Christmas. Can you save a present for me? I don't care what it is, it will be nice to have something new for when we move into a flat and I can look after things. Here at the hostel everything gets broken, or stolen, even the things that the Salvation Army give us.

You could give my Mum a present of some tissues with flowers on. She cries a lot and we walk in the park and flowers make her smile.

Thank you from Alicia.

PEGGY PRITCHARD'S CHRISTMAS

Sue Shattock

There was a single Christmas cracker
Beside the majestic portrait loved the most,
A half schooner of sweet sherry stood
Set ready for the toast.

She cut out shiny stars and tinsel
From foil with pinking shears.
Made an effort with the trifle,
Whilst holding back a well of tears.

Then sat, admired her handiwork,
And had a cup of tea
It was a sad lonely Christmas
And not yet half past three.

If she hadn't alienated the neighbours,
With the moans about their dog.
The inconsiderate parking
Or the annoying husband with brain fog.

If she'd only been more sociable,
Sympathetic instead of cross.
Then she might have had an invite out,
Never mind, it's all their loss.

Now the tinsel feels quite pointless,
The trifle much too bright.
Oh! The distant music and the laughter...
No! She'd have a very early night.

So, she gathered up her knitting.
And started up the stairs.
When a gentle knock upon her door
Caught her completely unawares.

A little boy, his name was Bruno,
Was shyly waiting just outside.
"Miss Pritchard, are you coming to our party?
It's going to be fun and dignified."

Well, she was shocked, delighted.
"Are you sure that you want me?'
'Yes, 'cos everyone likes parties
And there's roast turkey for our tea.

Did you get the invitation
That we popped in last week through the door?
You must have, you've made tinsel! Wow!
Can I help you make some more?"

She promised she'd be right along
With glue and pinking shears.
With rolls of foil and trifle,
Then overflowed with 'happy' tears.

The invite found, lost in a pile
Of bills and sad junk mail,
Read: Guest of honour, what a lark!
Now what would that entail?

She donned her greatest grandest dress
Some pearls, a cracker crown.
It made her smile to think of it,
Transformed her weary frown.

The party was a great success
And she the Christmas Queen.
They said: Your trifle is outstanding.
"It was the bestest, brightest ever seen."

And when the holiday was over,
With the old year in the past.
She had a treasure chest of memories,
And hopeful bridges built to last.

The neighbours, now friendly and familiar.
Invite Peggy regularly for tea.
And she teaches Bruno baking
And they have picnics by the sea.

The moral of this story is:
"If you get a second chance to shine
Be nice to all your neighbours
And make the most of Christmastime!"

Where's my hat? – Marcia White

THE CHRISTMAS SPECIAL

Sue Shattock

Mrs Padless and Buttercup are cooking in the kitchen at Upton Abbey. Mr Motley comes downstairs in a rush. The soup course has been served.

MOTLEY: Five minutes to mains Mrs P!

PADLESS: Buttercup!

MOTLEY His Lordship's telling one of his jokes.

BUTTERCUP: Did they like the soup?

MOTLEY: Fishing for compliments?

BUTTERCUP: No!

PADLESS: Pies need trimming and plating up. Come on girl, we haven't got all night!

MOTLEY: She's mooning over that new boyfriend of hers.

PADLESS: A new gentleman friend?

MOTLEY: Well, I shouldn't say really.

PADLESS: Buttercup! Get them pies out the oven and be quick about it.

BUTTERCUP: Yes, Mrs Padless.

PADLESS: Who?

MOTLEY: A lad from the village.

PADLESS: A new character?

MOTLEY: I can't say any more but it's all going to kick off in the Christmas special.

PADLESS: And my suggestion of our romantic entanglement?

MOTLEY: Apparently, it's a very packed episode.

PADLESS: *(disappointed)* Oh…. Well, she's a good girl. She deserves a decent story line.

MOTLEY: Don't we all.

PADLESS: Them carrots girl! They're boiling over!

BUTTERCUP: Sorry!

MOTLEY: You must be very proud of her.

PADLESS: She's keen enough.

MOTLEY: She could be so much more than just a cook.

PADLESS: There's nothing wrong with being a cook! I've been a cook for 42 years and just look at me.

BUTTERCUP: I can't find the garnishes! Where are the garnishes!

PADLESS: I've even got my own cookbook and they're featuring me in the Christmas edition of Good Housekeeping, with pictures, I had to get my hair done special.

MOTLEY: And very nice too, if I may say so.

PADLESS: Oh, Mr Motley!

MOTLEY: Ready to go?

PADLESS: I thought you'd never ask.

MOTLEY: What?

BUTTERCUP: I can't find the parsley sprinkles!

MOTLEY: The steak and ale pies, Mrs Padless?

PADLESS: Yes, of course, the pies. Clear
             Buttercup! Clear as you go.

BUTTERCUP: Garnishes, I can't find the
             garnishes!

PADLESS: Always keep your garnish basket
             to hand, not hidden away. Here
             you go - are these the ingredients
             for your soup?

BUTTERCUP: Yes, all freshly gathered per your
             instructions. Ow! These plates
             are bloody hot!

MOTLEY: Buttercup!

BUTTERCUP: Sorry Mr Motley.

PADLESS: Did you taste the soup before it
             was served Buttercup?

BUTTERCUP: Of course I did! You're such a
             fusser!

PADLESS: Oh. I'm so sorry.

MOTLEY: Buttercup!

BUTTERCUP: Well, she does my head in
             sometimes. I'm so looking
             forward to my very own
             storyline. I might even get a spin
             off series.

MOTLEY: "We are such stuff as dreams are made on"

BUTTERCUP: Don't tell me…. The Tempest Act 4 scene 1!

MOTLEY: Correct. Mrs Padless is anything the matter.

PADLESS: Them upstairs. They all loved Buttercup's soup?

MOTLEY: Clean plates. But they love everything that you do. You're a very popular character.   Lady Tulip's wedding cake. Well, that was sheer inspiration.

PADLESS: I think I'd better sit down.

BUTTERCUP: What about your special gravy?

PADLESS: No need for gravy.

MOLESELY: Are you feeling quite well Mrs Padless?

PADLESS: Wild mushroom with croutons and a drizzle of truffle oil.

BUTTERCUP: There's no need to take on so Mrs Padless, I can give you the recipe.

MOTLEY: It's gone very quiet up there.
            Lady Edie has probably dropped
            her bombshell.

BUTTERCUP: Not another one!

PADLESS: I'm afraid it's far more serious
            than that.

BUTTERCUP: Not twins!

MOTLEY: Christmas Special! I couldn't
            possibly say.

BUTTERCUP: I feel a bit sick.

PADLESS: I'm so sorry Buttercup there's
            nothing I can do. You never
            usually taste nothing.

BUTTERCUP: Aaargh!!! Mrs Padless!?

PADLESS: Wild mushrooms can be very
            tricky. This one looks as innocent
            as you like, but it's an easy
            mistake to make, you mustn't
            upset yourself.

MOTLEY: Mrs Padless?

PADLESS: Characters come and go that's all.
            It's perfectly natural.

MOTLEY: What have you done!

PADLESS: Me?   Nothing Mr Motley! *(she kisses him gently on the cheek).* Nothing at all... But I think this year's Christmas Special might feature the below stairs characters a little more than usual. And that will be a nice change, won't it.

She smiles to herself and checks her hairdo in her shiny spoon.

Christmas Table – Marcia White

THE BREATH INBETWEEN

Sue Shattock

In the breath between Christmas and New Year
There's a space betwixt darkness and light
Where opportunity knocks for a moment
To brighten our bone-weary night

The breathless bustle and hurry of Christmas
Gives a present to pause end of year
It's a blessing for those who embrace it
To be alone but complete without fear

And as the world keeps on in its turning
There are distractions galore if we look
But in the breath between
Christmas and New Year
It's okay to relax with a book.

Just Chillin' – Marcia White

ONWARD

Sue Shattock

Yes, time passes us on
Carelessly
Catapulting
Hapless humanity
Past Christmas
Into new orbits
Radiant with possibility

AVRIL'S NEW YEAR MULTIPLE CHOICE QUIZ

1. In which year did the Gregorian calendar replace the Julian calendar?
a)   1490
b)   1582
c)   1450

2. When is Chinese New Year?
a) First new moon of the Chinese Lunar Calendar
b) First full moon of the Chinese Lunar Calendar
c) 28 days after Gregorian New Year's Eve

3. What is Jewish New Year called?
a) Yom Kippur
b) Hanukkah
c) Rosh Hashana

4. Many Pagans celebrate the beginning of the new year on 31st October. What is the festival called?
a) Shaman
b) Samhain
c) Sanhina

5. Hindu New Year celebrates the triumph of light over darkness. What is the festival called?

a) Diwali

b) Holi

c) Rama Navami

6. In which country is it traditional to eat Lentils at New Year in the hope it will bring good fortune?

a) Chile

b) Brazil

c) Peru

7. In which country is it traditional to burn a scarecrow on New Year's eve?

a) Argentina

b) Peru

c) Ecuador

8. In which country is it traditional to dress up as a bear to chase away evil spirits at New Year?

a) Romania

b) Black Forest region of Germany

c) Slovakia

9. In which South African city do residents like to start the new year without any unwanted items and will traditionally throw old furniture out of a window?

a) Johannesburg

b) Cape Town

c) Durban

10. It is customary in Spain to welcome the New Year by:

a) Dancing on a table
b) Eating 12 grapes
c) Not drinking alcohol until the clock has struck midnight.

ANSWERS AT THE END OF THE BOOK

Is it next year yet? - Marcia White

A NEW YEAR REFLECTION

Nadya Henwood

This New Year's morning on the dog walk,
As I slowly trudged through the ice,
The dog snug in her winter coat,
Me wrapped up warm in woolly hat,
Cashmere scarf and thermal gloves;
I spotted an Adonis floating in the sea,
Basking, bare-chested, in the winter sun.

I thought, he'll freeze to death when he emerges!
But no, he walked nonchalantly up the beach,
His bright orange trunks, a beacon in the snow.
Then, to my surprise, he started exercising,
As children played in iced-up puddles alongside
him;
Stretches, sit-ups and press-ups, not a care in the
world,
While parents watched open-mouthed, in stunned
silence.

There and then, a chasm opened before my eyes,
Between the strength of youth and the fragility of
age,
The courage of man and vulnerability of woman.
We strive to be equal, but the same we are not.
Today, I envied his freedom. But tomorrow?
For him it's back to work, for me another dog
walk.
He will be trudging, and I will be free.

Keeping Cosy – Marcia White

TIME

Marcia White

What are we doing?

It's time to play:

I believe.

Time to love.

Time to venture.

Time to laugh.

Time to be gracious.

Time to live every moment.

Time to be the best we can.

Time to celebrate the sunrise.

Time to be thankful, as we watch the sun set.

PERFECT TIMING

Sue Shattock

Time tick-toc-ticks on tiptoe
Trickling gently into tomorrow
Fixed in the ever-changing moment
That is now
Capturing us within cascades of
Yesterday
Last Year
And I remember
Once upon a time...
Circles and cycles
Structure every everyday
Cycles and circles
The hopeful made-up journey
Of the round and round
Cementing the straight and narrow
Creating all our tomorrows
From the seeds of all our yesterdays
And in every single moment
A chance
An everlasting chance
To create it differently
Happy New Year!

Perfect Timing – Marcia White

FESTIVE CODEWORD SOLUTION

C	E	L	E	B	R	A	T	I	O	N	S	
H			E					A			
R	A	F	F	L	E	D		P		T	O	Y
I		A	L		A	I	R		I		
S	M				T	E	L	V	E	S	
T	W	I	N	K	L	E		S		I		A
M		L		I			E		T	I	N
A		Y	O	N		J	N		Y		T
S			G	R	O	T	T	O			A
	B	O	W	S		Y		S		N	
	O		I			O			O	
E	X	E	S		Q	U	I	Z	Z	E	S
			H			S			L	

1	2	3	4	5	6	7	8	9	10	11	12	
C	V	Y	H	J	M	E	P	S	B	D	Q	I
14	15	16	17	18	19	20	21	22	23	24	25	
N	L	W	T	X	G	U	A	K	O	Z	R	F

SOLUTIONS TO LIGHTING UP LONDON QUIZ

1	b	1978
2	a	1881
3	a	Regent Street
4	c	1954
5	c	5,000 hand painted Brussel Sprouts
6	a	1987
7	c	1947
8	c	Twice
9	b	Alladin
10	a	J M Barrie

SOLUTIONS TO NEW YEAR'S EVE QUIZ

1	b	1582
2	a	First full moon of Chinese lunar calendar
3	c	Rosh Hashana
4	b	Samhain
5	a	Diwalli
6	b	Italy
7	c	Ecuador
8	a	Romania
9	a	Johannesburg
10	b	Eating 12 grapes

THE RED TEAPOT COMPANY

Avril J Evitts started her writing career as a freelance journalist, concentrating on in-depth interviews and music reviews. She then followed an academic career, writing research proposals and papers. On retiring, Avril started to write fiction and her first book of short stories, Night Shift, was published in 2023. Avril's passions are swimming, live music and theatre. She lives on the West Sussex coast.

Ken Hawkins writes short plays and stories. He is also a voluntary presenter on hospital radio and a voluntary guide at a local museum dedicated to WWII. Ken is also involved in Green politics, having stood at local elections and the 2017 General Election. He enjoys reading modern history and is a fan of Nevil Shute, a novelist and engineer who designed and built aircraft at Portsmouth airport.

 **Nadya Henwood** writes, directs and performs poetry and plays. She has performed her poetry alongside Sue and directed her own plays, *Confession* and *Potted Pride and Prejudice* for Worthing Theatre Trail. Nadya has also acted in several local productions. Most recently, she directed her own full stage adaptation of *Pride and Prejudice* for Rustington Players. Nadya enjoys theatre, swimming, walking and travelling.

 Sue Shattock is a writer and marriage registrar. After a career as a stage manager in TV and theatre she went on to write scripts for *The Bill* and *Emmerdale*. Her first book *My Voice in Verse* is available on Amazon. Sue lives and works in Chichester and has recently completed her new booklet *Finding the Sunshine* a Cancer Journey in chapter and verse. She enjoys sharing and performing her work and writes about everyday things with a splash of humour and an infectious sense of fun.

Marcia White is a multidisciplinary artist and storyteller, whose practices include photography, playwriting and sculpture. Her training is in interior design. Marcia weaves vivid narratives that captivate both the eye and the imagination. Marcia's passions for travel and art fuel her creative pursuits, allowing her to capture and transform the beauty she encounters into various forms of artistic expression. She cherishes time spent with her family and friends, drawing inspiration from their support and experiences.